To Pelts Wood UP
11/7/21

Kent Rhymes

Edited By Megan Roberts

First published in Great Britain in 2018 by:

Young Writers
Remus House
Coltsfoot Drive
Peterborough
PE2 9BF
Telephone: 01733 890066
Website: www.youngwriters.co.uk

All Rights Reserved
Book Design by Ashley Janson
© Copyright Contributors 2018
SB ISBN 978-1-78896-749-5
Printed and bound in the UK by BookPrintingUK
Website: www.bookprintinguk.com
YB0372H

FOREWORD

Dear Reader,

Are you ready to get your thinking caps on to puzzle your way through this wonderful collection?

Young Writers' Little Riddlers competition set out to encourage young writers to create their own riddles. Their answers could be whatever or whoever their imaginations desired; from people to places, animals to objects, food to seasons. Riddles are a great way to further the children's use of poetic expression, including onomatopoeia and similes, as well as encourage them to 'think outside the box' by providing clues without giving the answer away immediately.

All of us here at Young Writers believe in the importance of inspiring young children to produce creative writing, including poetry, and we feel that seeing their own riddles in print will keep that creative spirit burning brightly and proudly.

We hope you enjoy riddling your way through this book as much as we enjoyed reading all the entries.

CONTENTS

Independent Entries

Kavilaya Karthik (6)	1
Ollie Keith Powell (7)	2

Bryony School, Rainham

Nozithelo Mafu (5)	3
Jamie Peacock (6)	4
Deborah Adeyemi (6)	5
Caitlin Etana Mukungunuwa (5)	6
Katie Elizabeth Hare (6)	7
George Twigg (6)	8
Tyler Whiteman (6)	9
Jadesola Olukoya (6)	10
Ernie Bendelow (6)	11
Jude Gribble (6)	12
Robert Reeves (5)	13
Luke Taruvinga (6)	14

Greatstone Primary School, Greatstone

Rubyrose Boorman (6)	15
Tilly Carpenter (6)	16
Katy Day (7)	17
Emilia Wilson-Lockyer (6)	18
Grace Hollett (6)	19
Evie Stafford (7)	20
Elle Chittenden (7)	21
Kamran Adam (7)	22
Alex Dennison (7)	23
Daniel George Challis (7)	24
Teddy Marriner-King (7)	25
Aisha Tariq (7)	26
Reece Oliver (7)	27

Keegan Gibbs (7)	28
Finley Hill (6)	29
Abbie Smith (7)	30
Callie Newman (7)	31
Jack Ostridge-King (7)	32
Jasmine Emily-Cleo Anderson-Hunt (7)	33
Ethan Oliver (6)	34
Alfie Jones (7)	35
Archie Benham (7)	36

Hurst Primary School, Bexley

Miley Dance (6)	37
Poppy Corley (6)	38
Alex Elias (6)	39
Jasmin Marshall (6)	40
Cameron Miller (6)	41
Ava Carr (6)	42
Maria Yalcin (6)	43
Teddy-James Wise (6)	44
Ava Charlton (5)	45
Sienna Ross (6)	46
Alivia Gore (6)	47
Lilly Grace Hewitt (6)	48
Ella Hopton (6)	49
Avaani Lola Chibber (6)	50
Josh Hoyle (6)	51
Kiyanah Aggrey-Amoah (5)	52
Noah Smith (6)	53
Freya Goldsmith (5)	54
Seb Blake-Bullock (5)	55
Elliot Graham Hughes (6)	56
Leah Bruce (6)	57
Gracie Rose Putnam (5)	58
Flynn Ethan Wallis (6)	59

Phoebe Joy Silley (5)	60
Emily Jenkins (6)	61
Behzod Raupov (6)	62
Lola Portch (6)	63
Samuel Leonard Lidbury (5)	64
Nathan Ramzan (6)	65

Priory Infant School, Ramsgate

Thomas Haddock (7)	66
Isabelle O'Dell Smith (7)	67
Kyla Downton (7)	68
Lenia Costello-Nichols (7)	69
Finley Hawkes (7)	70
Teagan Torbett-Bethune (6)	71
Jacob R A Fromage (7)	72
Marcus Cronin (7)	73
Oakly Simpson (6)	74
Chaz Plaice (6)	75
Charlie Martin (7)	76
Chloe Sackett (7)	77
Finley Edward Clark (6)	78
Adsayan Sarvanantharajah (7)	79
Chloe Anne Gardiner (7)	80
Summer Fraser (7)	81
Macie Mansfield (7)	82
David Stevens (7)	83
Skye Waldie-Temple (7)	84
Bella Skye Holbrook (7)	85
Alice Mary Elizabeth Lee West (7)	86
Parisa Daruwala (7)	87
Stephen Scott Lawrence (7)	88
Agata Piecuch (7)	89
Frankie Bateson (6)	90
Effie Price (7)	91
Daniel Mothersele (6)	92
Sienna Williams (6)	93
Atilas Augys (7)	94
Dylan Dickerson (6)	95
Amelia O'Sullivan (7)	96
Joshua Phoenix (7)	97
Maddison Lily Philpott (7)	98
Nancy Taheri (7)	99
Elsie Bassett-Cookson (6)	100
Poppy May Penney (7)	101
Kacee Lammin (7)	102
Alfie Clarke (7)	103
Millie Laplain-Emptage (7)	104
Curtis Overy (7)	105

Snodland CE Primary School, Snodland

Stephanie Walters (11)	106

St Crispin's Community Primary Infant School, Westgate

Caitlin Mountain (6)	107
Alivia Megan Fibbens (6)	108
Lola Dearnley (6)	109
Matilda Florrie Dolan (6)	110
Amy Parker-Webber (6)	111
Poppy May Spinner (6)	112
Lexi Kuhl (6)	113
Ellie-Mai Crosby (6)	114
Betsy Barnett (5)	115
Louie Cocks (6)	116

St Nicholas CE (VC) Infant School, Strood

Scarlett Robertson (7)	117
Anthony Curcio (7)	118
Mia Rose Townsend (7)	119
Ruby Killoran (7)	120
Jayden Bell (7)	121
Ryan Streatfield (7)	122
Taylor Popeley (7)	123
Isobel Green (7)	124
Kimberly Louise Sancto (6)	125
Stella Katie Thomas (7)	126
Harley Miller (7)	127
Danny Lewis Chambers (7)	128
Garvyn Sohal (7)	129
Louis Knight (7)	130
Leo Burdett (7)	131

Kian Reeves (7)	132
Jake Living (6)	133
Harvie-James Upton (7)	134

St Peter & St Paul Catholic Primary Academy, St Paul's Cray

James John Ruffle (6)	135
Caleb Olivier (6)	136
Isobelle Hobson McDonagh (6)	137
Jasmine Ellen Powell (6)	138
Mark Muthike Karimi (6)	139
Oliviia Barbashova (6)	140
Shi Yu Lin (6)	141
Camilla Ivy Maria Nangonzi Ssemanda (6)	142
Grace Knorton (6)	143
Lize-Mari Nel (6)	144
Michelle Stamerra (5)	145
Alfie Kerry (6)	146
Finley Hopkins (6)	147
Kiara Chin (6)	148
Henry Taylor (5)	149

Valley Invicta Primary School At Kings Hill, Kings Hill

Emilia Sophia Mirsadeghi (7)	150
Martin Neves Hajdinjak (7)	151
Cody Embery-Reid (7)	152
Rufaro Chihlayo	153
Luca Jack Hewlett (7)	154
Jasmine Lara	155
Thomas Miller	156
Alex Zilliox	157
Zachary Harding	158

Westgate Primary School, Dartford

Sydnee Mitchell (7)	159
Yasmine Rouabhi (7)	160
Solah Hayat (7)	161
Dumebi Lauren Molokwu (7)	162

Ire Sulaimon (7)	163
Ashwina Shagindra (7)	164
Rammiya Sathiyavarathan (7)	165
Nazeeha Noor Mohamed (7)	166
Callum Hardy (7)	167
Macey Poppy Manning (7)	168
Lola Cousins (6)	169
Prionti Kazi Munia (6)	170

Westmeads Community Infant School, Whitstable

Hester Liddicoat (6)	171

White Cliffs Primary College For The Arts, Dover

Ruby-Rae (6)	172
Kelsi H (6)	173
Zane Rackstraw (6)	174
Alexander Maneshi (6)	175
Grace Leigh Broster (6)	176
Eleanor-Rose Mctaggart (5)	177

THE POEMS

It's Everywhere

I am as blank as a piece of paper,
I am not coloured... just like water,
I hide in every crammed space,
Even in deserts!
Even in the ice!
I live everywhere in the world!
There's very little of me in the water and there's none of me in outer space.
You can't survive without me.
What am I?

Answer: Air.

Kavilaya Karthik (6)

Round Mound

I am round,
I get kicked a lot,
I get rolled a lot,
I get goals,
I am different colours,
I am very good at rolling,
What am I?

Answer: A football.

Ollie Keith Powell (7)

Desert Giant

I have dots like Mr Tumble,
I eat juicy leaves from trees,
I have pointy ears,
I live in African plains,
I am a child-bearing animal,
I like to rest in the shade from the burning sun,
What am I?

Answer: A giraffe.

Nozithelo Mafu (5)
Bryony School, Rainham

High Flyer

I am brown,
I can see in the dark like a wolf,
I make a noise like my mummy screaming,
I like to sit in the trees like a monkey,
I like to eat bugs like a spider,
I can fly like a fairy,
What am I?

Answer: An owl.

Jamie Peacock (6)
Bryony School, Rainham

Precious Plastic

I am as still as a tuatara.
I can be any beautiful colour.
You can buy me in a shop.
I am made out of plastic.
You can play with me to make you happy.
I can have long or short hair.
What am I?

Answer: A doll.

Deborah Adeyemi (6)
Bryony School, Rainham

Super Colour Creature

I have a long tail,
I live on rocks,
My feet are like hands,
My eyes are round and bulgy,
I can camouflage,
I walk in slow motion,
I look like a lizard in a tree,
What am I?

Answer: A chameleon.

Caitlin Etana Mukungunuwa (5)
Bryony School, Rainham

The Tail Chaser

I like to play outside,
I like to chase my tail,
I am as brown as chocolate,
My nose is as black as the stormy sky,
I like to sleep,
I like to chase cats,
What am I?

Answer: A dog.

Katie Elizabeth Hare (6)
Bryony School, Rainham

Banana Boo!

I itch my armpits,
I like to eat bananas like a minion,
I live in a jungle,
I like to swing in trees,
I drop banana splits,
I sit in trees,
What am I?

Answer: A gorilla.

George Twigg (6)
Bryony School, Rainham

Sssuper Tongue

I am as long as a metal pole,
I am poisonous,
I live on the biggest island in the world,
I am as brown as mud,
I bite you,
I am slimy,
What am I?

Answer: A snake.

Tyler Whiteman (6)
Bryony School, Rainham

Happy Feet

I live in the coldest continent,
I swim in the sea,
I have black and white skin,
I have flat arms,
I cannot speak,
I have two eyes,
What am I?

Answer: A penguin.

Jadesola Olukoya (6)
Bryony School, Rainham

Little Brown Nut

I collect nuts and acorns,
I am silky brown in colour,
I hibernate in the winter,
I have a long, bushy tail,
I live in the trees,
What am I?

Answer: A squirrel.

Ernie Bendelow (6)
Bryony School, Rainham

Fluffy Brown

I have brown skin,
I am a mammal,
I eat meat,
I have fluffy fur,
I like to eat delicious honey,
I am as big as a lorry,
What am I?

Answer: A bear.

Jude Gribble (6)
Bryony School, Rainham

Claw Fighter

I can jump really far,
I can run really fast,
I am as orange as a red squirrel,
I have very sharp teeth,
I have got hair,
What am I?

Answer: A lion.

Robert Reeves (5)
Bryony School, Rainham

Jungle King

I can run as fast as a dog,
I roar as loud as a dinosaur,
My paws are stripy like a bee,
I am the king of the jungle,
What am I?

Answer: A tiger.

Luke Taruvinga (6)
Bryony School, Rainham

What Is It?

It looks pink,
It has a beak,
It has blue eyes like a pet,
It lives in a jungle,
It doesn't hate you,
It is nice,
It flies
It is slow,
You can't make it run, or it will bite,
They are so furry, you will want to sleep on them,
What is it?

Answer: A flamingo.

Rubyrose Boorman (6)
Greatstone Primary School, Greatstone

Secret Big Animal

They look cute, but will bite you,
They are the fastest animal on land,
They live in grass and play in grass,
What's special about them is that they are famous because they can run faster than a person, animal, or stuff in the sea like a crocodile.
What are they?

Answer: Cheetahs.

Tilly Carpenter (6)
Greatstone Primary School, Greatstone

Oh! It's A Secret

I'm a mammal,
I have monstrous tusks,
You may like me,
I squirt water,
I live in Africa,
I tie knots in a part of my body,
You shouldn't hug me,
I have big ears that hear from miles away,
I might have muddy feet,
What am I?

Answer: An elephant.

Katy Day (7)
Greatstone Primary School, Greatstone

165 Million Years Ago

They hide to catch their prey,
They have teeth as sharp as knives,
They have claws so sharp, you will faint,
They eat meat,
They lived 165 million years ago,
They roar so loudly, they would blow you off your feet,
What are they?

Answer: Dinosaurs.

Emilia Wilson-Lockyer (6)
Greatstone Primary School, Greatstone

Grey Mountain Animal

My animal is a herbivore,
It is huge and very big,
It has a long nose but doesn't talk with it,
It makes quite a noise,
It has a loud voice,
Sometimes, it makes large footprints,
It has a smooth body,
What is it?

Answer: An elephant.

Grace Hollett (6)
Greatstone Primary School, Greatstone

What Is It?

It has long teeth and sharp claws,
It lives in grasslands,
It eats lots of meat every single day,
It is so fluffy,
Its roar can be heard five miles away,
If it bites you, you can die,
What is it?

Answer: A tiger.

Evie Stafford (7)
Greatstone Primary School, Greatstone

Nibbles On Wood

I'm very light,
I've got massive ears,
I've got a big body,
I've got one eye on each side,
I've got four feet,
I like to exercise,
I have only one tooth,
What am I?

Answer: A hamster.

Elle Chittenden (7)
Greatstone Primary School, Greatstone

What Am I?

I hunt people down,
I eat plants,
I am fast,
I have feathers,
I have a small head,
My eggs are larger than chickens' ones,
I'm fluffy,
I have two legs,
What am I?

Answer: An ostrich.

Kamran Adam (7)
Greatstone Primary School, Greatstone

What Is It?

It has a long tongue,
It's a pack hunter,
It's a carnivore,
It has big ears that hear faraway predators behind the trees,
Its roar can be heard from five miles away,
What is it?

Answer: A lion.

Alex Dennison (7)
Greatstone Primary School, Greatstone

Big And Small

I'm grumpy and I feel dumpy,
I'm very big,
I definitely won't dig,
I'm a herbivore,
I eat leaves,
I climb trees,
I look wonky,
But I'm not a donkey!

Answer: A gorilla.

Daniel George Challis (7)
Greatstone Primary School, Greatstone

What Is It?

It is really heavy,
It sprays water,
It is big,
It is fat,
It is a herbivore and eats leaves,
It has a floppy trunk,
It has a big, hairy, fluffy tail,
What is it?

Answer: An elephant.

Teddy Marriner-King (7)
Greatstone Primary School, Greatstone

Secret Animals Riddle

It is a wild animal,
It lives in Africa,
It's a herbivore,
It loves to eat vegetables,
You will see it in the zoo,
It has a monstrously tough trunk,
What is it?

Answer: An elephant.

Aisha Tariq (7)
Greatstone Primary School, Greatstone

What Is It?

It's stripy,
It's an animal,
It's furry,
It can be seen by anyone in the world,
It has a wavy tail,
It is black and white,
What is it?

Answer: A zebra.

Reece Oliver (7)
Greatstone Primary School, Greatstone

Flying Creature

I live by the sea,
I fly,
I make a lot of noise,
I have feathers,
I sit on houses,
I'm a two-legged creature,
What am I?

Answer: A seagull.

Keegan Gibbs (7)
Greatstone Primary School, Greatstone

What Is It?

It has four legs.
It has four paws.
It has two eyes
And might have brown fur.
It has a tail.
It's like a wolf.
What is it?

Answer: A dog.

Finley Hill (6)
Greatstone Primary School, Greatstone

What Is It?

It has stripes,
It eats meat,
It has sharp claws,
It can be big and small,
It lives in the jungle,
It is fierce,
What is it?

Answer: A tiger.

Abbie Smith (7)
Greatstone Primary School, Greatstone

King Of The Prey

It flies in the sky,
It is large and powerful,
It has very good eyes,
It is called a bird of prey,
It is very fast,
What is it?

Answer: An eagle.

Callie Newman (7)
Greatstone Primary School, Greatstone

What Am I?

I have sharp, pointy teeth,
I am a carnivore,
I am stripy,
I can run fast and can run about 30mph,
I am scary,
What am I?

Answer: A tiger.

Jack Ostridge-King (7)
Greatstone Primary School, Greatstone

Predator Power!

I am a predator,
I am cute,
I am the baby of an animal,
I am small,
I hate dogs,
I may scratch you,
What am I?

Answer: A kitten.

Jasmine Emily-Cleo Anderson-Hunt (7)
Greatstone Primary School, Greatstone

What Am I?

I spray water,
I am fat,
I am heavy,
I'm a herbivore,
I hate lions,
I make noise,
What am I?

Answer: An elephant.

Ethan Oliver (6)
Greatstone Primary School, Greatstone

What Is It?

It eats people,
It goes hunting on its own,
It eats herds,
It eats meat,
It is scaly,
What is it?

Answer: A crocodile.

Alfie Jones (7)
Greatstone Primary School, Greatstone

What Is It?

It is small,
It goes in mud,
It is strong,
It is small like a rock,
It has lots of legs,
What is it?

Answer: An ant.

Archie Benham (7)
Greatstone Primary School, Greatstone

Sticky, Slimy Riddle

I move very slowly,
I go pretty much everywhere,
I like to eat crunchy leaves,
When I am tired, I find a comfy place to go to sleep,
It has to be a safe place too,
I am usually by myself, but I do have a family,
I am bigger than an ant,
I live in a shell, but it has to be hard to protect me from other animals,
I'm as small as a cup,
What am I?

Answer: A snail.

Miley Dance (6)
Hurst Primary School, Bexley

The Shell Riddle

I live in a shell and sometimes I curl up in my shell,
I'm as small as a rock,
I am bigger than a pound coin,
I can make slime and move about,
I have no legs,
I like to hide on the glittery leaves,
I go everywhere in the world, inside as well,
I come out when it's raining,
People step on me sometimes,
Sometimes I am alone,
What am I?

Answer: A snail.

Poppy Corley (6)
Hurst Primary School, Bexley

The Mystery Bug

I have patterned wings and I taste with my feet,
I sometimes sting other people if they distract me,
I have four parts of me,
I sleep in a cone for a month,
I look like a colourful moth flying high, doing loop-the-loops,
I like flying near other friendly animals,
I'm as wide as a hand,
I'm smaller than a blank tissue,
What am I?

Answer: A butterfly.

Alex Elias (6)
Hurst Primary School, Bexley

The Shiny Dragonflies

I fly high in the sky,
I like to whizz around in hot places near ponds that are huge,
I have two wings that are huge and big,
I must sleep in the water for ten years,
I eat tadpoles and they're yummy,
I am bigger than ten pence,
I am as long as a pencil,
I'm usually in hot places,
I live near ponds,
What am I?

Answer: A dragonfly.

Jasmin Marshall (6)
Hurst Primary School, Bexley

Colourful Bug Puzzle

I can wriggle, but I'm underground,
I must hide from birds otherwise they eat me,
I hide in my dirty soil cave,
I make tricky, hard tunnels in my muck,
I get tired when I'm finished,
I'm smaller than a tiny pin,
I'm pink and I'm extremely dirty,
I don't like it when the earth shakes,
What am I?

Answer: A worm.

Cameron Miller (6)
Hurst Primary School, Bexley

Wriggly Riddle

I can fly like a moth,
I like nectar and sticky pollen,
I live anywhere,
Sometimes, I fly over trees,
I go to flowers to get nectar,
I'm usually found on yummy flowers,
I have curly antennae,
I have a black body,
My wings flutter and flap,
People call me flutterby,
I've got colourful wings,
What am I?

Answer: A butterfly.

Ava Carr (6)
Hurst Primary School, Bexley

Fly!

I have eyes under my wings,
I flutter my wings 200 times in the glorious, blue sky,
I am beautiful when I'm in the burning sun,
I live in bumpy, green trees,
When my tummy rumbles, I collect pollen and nectar from enormous flowers,
I fly,
I am fast,
What am I?

Answer: A butterfly.

Maria Yalcin (6)
Hurst Primary School, Bexley

Lovely Lady

I lay yellow eggs,
I have two pairs of wings,
I have three thin legs on each side,
I don't like the freezing cold, frosty weather,
I like to live near beautiful, sweet smelling flowers,
My favourite food is aphids,
I am red and black,
What am I?

Answer: A ladybird.

Teddy-James Wise (6)
Hurst Primary School, Bexley

Royalty

I can live for four or five years,
I am in charge of all the workers who make yummy food for the babies,
I am a very important insect,
I am the biggest in my colony,
You will hear me coming,
I have a very fluffy, soft body,
What am I?

Answer: A queen bee.

Ava Charlton (5)
Hurst Primary School, Bexley

Wings

Even though I am beautiful, I am disgusting to eat,
I have no mouth, but I taste with my feet,
I have a long, black tongue and my antennae are quite long,
I look so beautiful when I fly,
People used to call me flutterby,
What am I?

Answer: A butterfly.

Sienna Ross (6)
Hurst Primary School, Bexley

Sun Bright

My wings are not joined together,
Sometimes I look like a leaf,
My front wings do most of the work,
I don't have a mouth, but I have a long tongue,
The dark parts of my wings warm me up,
I taste with my feet,
What am I?

Answer: A butterfly.

Alivia Gore (6)
Hurst Primary School, Bexley

Flying

I taste with my feet,
I go through metamorphosis,
I don't have a mouth, but drink with a long, slimy tongue,
I normally lay eggs on food plants,
I am beautiful,
People used to call me flutterby,
What am I?

Answer: A butterfly.

Lilly Grace Hewitt (6)
Hurst Primary School, Bexley

Hairy Body

I am everywhere,
I'm sometimes in your garden,
I am small and round,
My legs are as skinny as a mouse's tail,
Sometimes I hide in your bushes,
I can make my own silky house,
I am black,
What am I?

Answer: A spider.

Ella Hopton (6)
Hurst Primary School, Bexley

Fuzzy Friends

We talk to our friends by dancing,
We can be found all over the world,
Not all of us have yellow stripes,
Drones are the names of the males,
We have two legs in front of our eyes,
If we sting, we die,
What are we?

Answer: Bees.

Avaani Lola Chibber (6)
Hurst Primary School, Bexley

Fast Fly!

I can go underwater for a year,
I have 30,000 thin lenses,
I have colossal eyes,
I have shiny, crystal wings,
I was on the earth before the dinosaurs,
I can be beautiful blue and perfect pink,
What am I?

Answer: A dragonfly.

Josh Hoyle (6)
Hurst Primary School, Bexley

Lovely Man

I move very slowly,
I lay 100 eggs,
I only like places that are damp,
I have four, long tentacles on top of my head,
I leave slime wherever I go,
I live in a shell,
I like eating lettuce,
What am I?

Answer: A snail.

Kiyanah Aggrey-Amoah (5)
Hurst Primary School, Bexley

Honey Licker

I live in a jungle, and maybe a forest,
I love honey but I'm not a bunny,
I am stronger than a daddy lion,
I have a furry body,
I am big, but never small,
I have a wet, black nose,
What am I?

Answer: A bear.

Noah Smith (6)
Hurst Primary School, Bexley

Small But Deadly

I am very strong,
I live in every corner of the world,
I am sometimes black and sometimes red,
I have two antennae,
I bite most of the time,
People may say I'm small,
What am I?

Answer: An ant.

Freya Goldsmith (5)
Hurst Primary School, Bexley

Grass Creature

I can jump twenty times my length,
I make beautiful noises with my legs,
I have two sets of speedy wings and have small eyes,
I have two antennae,
I am great and green,
What am I?

Answer: A grasshopper.

Seb Blake-Bullock (5)
Hurst Primary School, Bexley

Wriggly

I can't move quickly,
I eat light green leaves,
I sometimes have spots on me,
I might be bright, but I am disgusting,
I am hairy,
I turn into a butterfly,
What am I?

Answer: A caterpillar.

Elliot Graham Hughes (6)
Hurst Primary School, Bexley

Flappy

I don't have a mouth,
I can fly,
I drink with my long tongue,
The dark parts of my wings warm up quickly,
I am the biggest fly,
I am pretty and little,
What am I?

Answer: A butterfly.

Leah Bruce (6)
Hurst Primary School, Bexley

Slimy

I am no bigger than cherries,
I live in damp places,
I am a boy and a girl,
I am a type of mollusc,
My body is squishy,
I need lots of moisture to survive,
What am I?

Answer: A snail.

Gracie Rose Putnam (5)
Hurst Primary School, Bexley

Fly Killer

I have to be kept on my own, or I will eat other things like me,
I can be as big as a plate,
I can blend in,
I have eight eyes,
I have eight long, slim legs,
What am I?

Answer: A spider.

Flynn Ethan Wallis (6)
Hurst Primary School, Bexley

Sky

I taste with my feet,
I drink a sweet liquid,
I may have hundreds of eggs inside me,
I go through metamorphosis,
I have dark parts on me,
I can fly,
What am I?

Answer: A butterfly.

Phoebe Joy Silley (5)
Hurst Primary School, Bexley

Beautiful Insects

I taste with my feet,
I used to be called flutterby,
I drink with a long tongue,
I don't have a mouth,
I have the same colours on both sides,
What am I?

Answer: A butterfly.

Emily Jenkins (6)
Hurst Primary School, Bexley

Hairy Insects

I can grow a new leg,
I have a head and a thorn,
I am not an insect,
I eat flies,
I have eight legs,
I trap flies with my tremendous webs,
What am I?

Answer: A spider.

Behzod Raupov (6)
Hurst Primary School, Bexley

What Am I?

I am fluffy and I do not like rain
I am little
I can fly
I have a sharp sting
I do like nectar
I do like making things with nectar
What am I?

Answer: A bee.

Lola Portch (6)
Hurst Primary School, Bexley

Spotty Lady

I don't like the freezing cold,
My eggs are yellow,
I have two pairs of wings,
I like to live in lovely gardens,
What am I?

Answer: A ladybird.

Samuel Leonard Lidbury (5)
Hurst Primary School, Bexley

The Man In A Can

I am hard,
I have a shell,
I am little,
I have fourteen legs,
I have a sting,
What am I?

Answer: A woodlouse.

Nathan Ramzan (6)
Hurst Primary School, Bexley

Bouncer

I like carrots,
I look like a bouncer,
I jump around a lot,
I live in a hutch,
I am as soft as a cat,
I like to hide and be cheeky,
I am a kind of animal,
What am I?

Answer: A rabbit.

Thomas Haddock (7)
Priory Infant School, Ramsgate

Fizzle

I have a long trunk,
I walk all day,
If you come too close, I might give you a splash,
I wiggle my tail when flies are around,
I give my babies a wash,
What am I?

Answer: An elephant.

Isabelle O'Dell Smith (7)
Priory Infant School, Ramsgate

What Am I?

I live in the North Pole,
I love eating carrots,
I have four legs,
I love my antlers because they're like trees,
I have thin, brown fur,
What am I?

Answer: A reindeer.

Kyla Downton (7)
Priory Infant School, Ramsgate

Furry

I am the king of the jungle,
I am fierce and hairy,
I have a huge mane,
I eat meat,
I move pretty fast,
I have babies called cubs,
What am I?

Answer: A lion.

Lenia Costello-Nichols (7)
Priory Infant School, Ramsgate

Munchy

I eat leaves,
I have long, long legs,
I also have big, brown spots,
I am as tall as a tree,
I love to eat stems from a tree,
What am I?

Answer: A giraffe.

Finley Hawkes (7)
Priory Infant School, Ramsgate

Stompy

I am really, really big,
I like to eat bark and leaves,
I have big, flappy ears,
I move quite loudly,
I look really tall,
What am I?

Answer: An elephant.

Teagan Torbett-Bethune (6)
Priory Infant School, Ramsgate

What Am I?

I have two ears on top of my head,
I love to wag my tail,
I bark when someone knocks at the door,
I like to eat bone-shaped biscuits,
What am I?

Answer: A dog

Jacob R A Fromage (7)
Priory Infant School, Ramsgate

Spiky

I am really, really spiky,
I do not stab,
I am not that big,
I like to hide in your garden,
I look like a spiky stone,
What am I?

Answer: A hedgehog.

Marcus Cronin (7)
Priory Infant School, Ramsgate

Honey Lover

I like sweet honey,
There are lots of types of me,
I am very furry,
I'm as loud as a tiger,
I've got piggy eyes,
What am I?

Answer: A bear.

Oakly Simpson (6)
Priory Infant School, Ramsgate

Stripe

I can sting you,
If I sting you, I die,
I have black and yellow stripes,
I have a small stinger,
I am big and squishy,
What am I?

Answer: A bee.

Chaz Plaice (6)
Priory Infant School, Ramsgate

The Meat Lover

I love meat,
I have a funny mane,
I come out at night,
I move like a cheetah,
I roar as loud as a tiger,
What am I?

Answer: A lion.

Charlie Martin (7)
Priory Infant School, Ramsgate

What Am I?

I have cute little ears,
I have lettuce for dinner,
I have five claws on each foot,
I have lots of fur,
What am I?

Answer: A guinea pig.

Chloe Sackett (7)
Priory Infant School, Ramsgate

Hives

I only have six legs,
I always sting you,
I live in hives,
I fly quickly and I'm a spy,
I eat honey,
What am I?

Answer: A bee.

Finley Edward Clark (6)
Priory Infant School, Ramsgate

What Am I?

I have black blobs,
I can climb trees,
I have sharp claws,
I have four legs,
I'm covered in fur,
What am I?

Answer: A leopard

Adsayan Sarvanantharajah (7)
Priory Infant School, Ramsgate

Fluffy

I can see in the dark,
I have wings,
I only come out at night,
I fly around at night,
I have big eyes,
What am I?

Answer: An owl.

Chloe Anne Gardiner (7)
Priory Infant School, Ramsgate

Cheeky

I hang on my mum,
I hunt for my food,
I live in a forest,
I love bananas,
I like to hang on a tree,
What am I?

Answer: A monkey.

Summer Fraser (7)
Priory Infant School, Ramsgate

Furry

I can see in the dark,
I have whiskers and long eyelashes,
I am small,
I have a tail,
I love Dreamies,
What am I?

Answer: A cat.

Macie Mansfield (7)
Priory Infant School, Ramsgate

Waddles

I like fish,
I waddle all the time,
I like swimming,
I live in Antarctica,
I'm a bird,
What am I?

Answer: A penguin.

David Stevens (7)
Priory Infant School, Ramsgate

Snappy

I eat meat,
I live in water,
I have sharp teeth,
I crawl on my feet,
I like to hunt,
What am I?

Answer: A crocodile.

Skye Waldie-Temple (7)
Priory Infant School, Ramsgate

What Am I?

I live in the zoo,
I like to hang upside down,
I am very noisy,
I eat ripe, yellow bananas,
What am I?

Answer: A monkey.

Bella Skye Holbrook (7)
Priory Infant School, Ramsgate

What Am I?

I live in a cave,
I have four feet but sometimes use two,
I am brave and large,
I love honey,
What am I?

Answer: A bear.

Alice Mary Elizabeth Lee West (7)
Priory Infant School, Ramsgate

What Am I?

I've got sharp teeth,
I swim in the ocean,
I am blue and white,
I eat sea creatures,
What am I?

Answer: A shark.

Parisa Daruwala (7)
Priory Infant School, Ramsgate

Munch

I have sharp teeth,
I have a tail,
I eat fish,
I swim in the sea,
I might eat you,
What am I?

Answer: A shark.

Stephen Scott Lawrence (7)
Priory Infant School, Ramsgate

What Am I?

I am good at running,
I have dots on me,
I hunt for food,
I run as fast as a rocket,
What am I?

Answer: A cheetah.

Agata Piecuch (7)
Priory Infant School, Ramsgate

What Am I?

I live in the South Pole,
I hunt for fish,
I have a white belly,
Orcas hunt for me,
What am I?

Answer: A penguin.

Frankie Bateson (6)
Priory Infant School, Ramsgate

Fluffy

I have a tall neck,
I eat plants and leaves from trees,
I have an orange and brown coat,
What am I?

Answer: A giraffe.

Effie Price (7)
Priory Infant School, Ramsgate

What Am I?

I live in hot places,
I love playing in the mud,
I have heavy fur,
I have a snout,
What am I?

Answer: A warthog.

Daniel Mothersele (6)
Priory Infant School, Ramsgate

What Am I?

I have two legs,
I have hair on my head,
I live in a house,
I eat all kinds of food,
What am I?

Answer: A human.

Sienna Williams (6)
Priory Infant School, Ramsgate

What Am I?

I have fur,
I make a squeaky sound,
I have flippers,
I have two wings,
What am I?

Answer: A duckling.

Atilas Augys (7)
Priory Infant School, Ramsgate

What Am I?

I am found in gardens,
I like fish,
I have sharp claws,
I am quite quiet,
What am I?

Answer: A cat.

Dylan Dickerson (6)
Priory Infant School, Ramsgate

What Am I?

I have four legs,
I'm covered in fur,
You might stroke me,
I go woof,
What am I?

Answer: A dog.

Amelia O'Sullivan (7)
Priory Infant School, Ramsgate

What Am I?

I live in a zoo,
I am grey,
I can break walls,
I have a horn,
What am I?

Answer: A rhinoceros.

Joshua Phoenix (7)
Priory Infant School, Ramsgate

What Am I?

I can fly,
I hang upside down at night,
I can give you a vampire bite,
What am I?

Answer: A bat.

Maddison Lily Philpott (7)
Priory Infant School, Ramsgate

What Am I?

I live in Africa,
I have black and white skin,
I have hooves,
What am I?

Answer: A zebra.

Nancy Taheri (7)
Priory Infant School, Ramsgate

What Am I?

I live in trees,
I have a fluffy tail,
I love to eat nuts,
What am I?

Answer: A squirrel.

Elsie Bassett-Cookson (6)
Priory Infant School, Ramsgate

Fluffy

I live in a zoo,
I have long hair,
I have hair like an orange,
What am I?

Answer: A lion.

Poppy May Penney (7)
Priory Infant School, Ramsgate

What Am I?

I am slimy,
I can jump high,
I am slippery,
I am green,
What am I?

Answer: A frog.

Kacee Lammin (7)
Priory Infant School, Ramsgate

Stitch

I eat grass,
I have a woolly coat,
I make a funny sound,
What am I?

Answer: A sheep.

Alfie Clarke (7)
Priory Infant School, Ramsgate

What Am I?

I walk,
I eat leaves,
I am big,
I have a long neck,
What am I?

Answer: A giraffe.

Millie Laplain-Emptage (7)
Priory Infant School, Ramsgate

Fierce

I roar,
I have brown stripes,
I am very fierce,
What am I?

Answer: A tiger.

Curtis Overy (7)
Priory Infant School, Ramsgate

Accessory

I come in different colours and styles,
I can be magnetic,
I have no front so you can see the screen,
But sometimes, if I close, you can't,
What am I?

Answer: A phone case.

Stephanie Walters (11)
Snodland CE Primary School, Snodland

What Am I?

I have two feet,
I have very small arms,
When I stamp my feet, the earth shakes,
When I get hungry, I kill the other dinosaurs,
I eat them with my sharp teeth,
I am sometimes green or red or plain grey,
I sometimes have lines on me,
What am I?

Answer: A T-rex.

Caitlin Mountain (6)
St Crispin's Community Primary Infant School, Westgate

What Am I?

I have a small head,
I'm not a carnivore,
I have four legs,
I have a long neck,
I am blue,
I have a small brain,
I have small eyes,
I do not have spots,
I have a small mouth,
My tail is big,
What am I?

Answer: A brachiosaurus.

Alivia Megan Fibbens (6)
St Crispin's Community Primary Infant School, Westgate

What Am I?

I am blue,
I live in the sea,
I have a very, very long neck,
I have small marks,
I have a little head,
I have a tiny tail,
I can go deep underwater,
I have little eyes,
I like underwater dinosaurs,
What am I?

Answer: A plesiosaur.

Lola Dearnley (6)
St Crispin's Community Primary Infant School, Westgate

The Green Dinosaur

I have a small brain,
I have a small tail,
I am green,
I have plates,
My plates are round and green,
I like plants, that means I'm a herbivore,
I have small legs,
I have small eyes,
What am I?

Answer: A stegosaurus.

Matilda Florrie Dolan (6)
St Crispin's Community Primary Infant School, Westgate

What Am I?

I am taller than two buses,
I am blue,
I have a very, very long neck,
I am a herbivore,
My legs are like marshmallows,
I have a little brain,
When I stomp my feet, the floor cracks,
What am I?

Answer: A brachiosaurus.

Amy Parker-Webber (6)
St Crispin's Community Primary Infant School, Westgate

The Herbivore

I am a herbivore,
I have three horns on my head,
My beak is like a parrot's,
I am white or grey,
My tail is short,
My feet have claws,
I am a dinosaur,
What am I?

Answer: A *triceratops*.

Poppy May Spinner (6)
St Crispin's Community Primary Infant School, Westgate

What Am I?

I have a really tall neck,
I have a very small brain,
I am blue and I am tall,
I am a herbivore,
I have very small eyes,
I am taller than two buses,
What am I?

Answer: A brachiosaurus.

Lexi Kuhl (6)
St Crispin's Community Primary Infant School, Westgate

What Am I?

I am red,
I have big claws and small claws,
I am a good runner,
I am terrifying and small,
I have pointy claws,
I have sharp teeth,
What am I?

Answer: A velociraptor.

Ellie-Mai Crosby (6)
St Crispin's Community Primary Infant School, Westgate

What Am I?

I am blue,
I have a very, very long neck,
I have a really long tail,
My feet look like elephant feet,
When I walk, the ground wobbles,
What am I?

Answer: A brachiosaurus.

Betsy Barnett (5)
St Crispin's Community Primary Infant School, Westgate

What Am I?

I am as big as a hippo,
I ambush my prey,
I like meat,
I can camouflage,
I have a pointy tail,
I can run faster than you,
What am I?

Answer: A velociraptor.

Louie Cocks (6)
St Crispin's Community Primary Infant School, Westgate

Hidden In A Bush

I hide in the bushes and fields,
I have six or more black spots,
I'm really lovely and kind,
I am red, black, and I love lettuce leaves,
I'm a little bit common,
I love wild places like gardens and corners with grass,
You don't see me often,
What am I?

Answer: A ladybird.

Scarlett Robertson (7)
St Nicholas CE (VC) Infant School, Strood

Mushroom Kingdom

I have a helper called Cappy,
I hate the Broodals,
My worst enemy is Bowser,
I travel in the Odyssey,
I find Power Moons,
I need suits to get into secret places,
I turn into people,
I have a brother called Luigi,
I can go into pipes,
Who am I?

Answer: Mario.

Anthony Curcio (7)
St Nicholas CE (VC) Infant School, Strood

Jumping Trees

I am furry and big and live in a jungle,
I love eating leaves and vegetables,
I jump around trees, swinging with my tail,
I have to go down my slide lots,
I can be brown with a white face,
People think I can be very cheeky,
What am I?

Answer: A monkey.

Mia Rose Townsend (7)
St Nicholas CE (VC) Infant School, Strood

Captain Of The Sky

I am everywhere and nowhere, many and few,
Look high or look low, it's really up to you,
I'm born in a pond then take to the sky,
I am five centimetres long,
You see me on hot, sunny days,
I am green or blue,
What am I?

Answer: A dragonfly.

Ruby Killoran (7)
St Nicholas CE (VC) Infant School, Strood

In A Forest

I am a big, soft, furry animal,
I can live in a cage or a zoo,
I eat fish and meat,
I can be in the wild forest,
I am usually brown,
Sometimes I get my fish from the lake or river,
I growl in a grizzly way,
What am I?

Answer: A bear.

Jayden Bell (7)
St Nicholas CE (VC) Infant School, Strood

Tree

I can be small, medium, or big,
I live outside or inside,
I can be black, brown, or yellow,
I find it easy to climb,
I can be hairy and scary,
I scuttle around and very quickly,
I make webs,
What am I?

Answer: A spider.

Ryan Streatfield (7)
St Nicholas CE (VC) Infant School, Strood

Who Am I?

I say tra-la-la,
I turn into him when someone snaps their fingers,
I turn back when I get water on me,
I've been in thirteen books,
I wear a cape to fly,
I wear underpants,
Who am I?

Answer: Captain Underpants.

Taylor Popeley (7)
St Nicholas CE (VC) Infant School, Strood

Inside Our Cage

People like to keep me as a pet,
I'm funny and like to eat vegetables,
People love me,
I squeak when the fridge opens,
I love warm baths to keep me clean,
I have four legs,
What am I?

Answer: A guinea pig.

Isobel Green (7)
St Nicholas CE (VC) Infant School, Strood

Flying In The Sky In Towns

I can fly in the sky and I've got two feet,
I've got feathers and I am grey,
I can peck you,
I am greedy,
People don't like me,
I like to eat seeds,
What am I?

Answer: A pigeon.

Kimberly Louise Sancto (6)
St Nicholas CE (VC) Infant School, Strood

I Am In A Tree

I am small and I have little legs,
I live in the garden in summer,
I have two wings so I can fly,
I can be red and black,
I have spots,
I enjoy aphids,
What am I?

Answer: A ladybird.

Stella Katie Thomas (7)
St Nicholas CE (VC) Infant School, Strood

What Am I, Guess?

I am yellow and not tasty,
People don't like me that much,
I am a food and I am a fruit,
I am sour,
I can be in a sweet,
I am not sweet,
What am I?

Answer: A lemon.

Harley Miller (7)
St Nicholas CE (VC) Infant School, Strood

Danny Chambers

I have black spots on my fur,
I like to eat hay,
People drink liquid from me,
I say, "Moo!"
I have a red tongue,
I like to moo,
What am I?

Answer: A cow.

Danny Lewis Chambers (7)
St Nicholas CE (VC) Infant School, Strood

Climbing

I live outside in the jungle,
I have two legs and arms,
I can be black and grey,
I eat meat,
I have sharp teeth,
I thump my chest,
What am I?

Answer: A gorilla.

Garvyn Sohal (7)
St Nicholas CE (VC) Infant School, Strood

Can't Move

I can't move,
I am really big,
I am not colourful,
I watch over the world,
I love you all,
I forgive bad people,
What am I?

Answer: The Statue of Liberty.

Louis Knight (7)
St Nicholas CE (VC) Infant School, Strood

Go Everywhere

I fall when little children are on me,
I have brakes for stopping,
I have pedals to make me go,
I have two wheels,
What am I?

Answer: A bike.

Leo Burdett (7)
St Nicholas CE (VC) Infant School, Strood

What Am I?

I have no legs,
I am a scaly reptile,
I am really black,
I have some venom,
I am creepy,
What am I?

Answer: A black mamba.

Kian Reeves (7)
St Nicholas CE (VC) Infant School, Strood

Hunt In A Hall

I have eight legs,
I have eight eyes,
I can see in the dark,
I have two fangs,
I can be big,
What am I?

Answer: A spider.

Jake Living (6)
St Nicholas CE (VC) Infant School, Strood

Scary Black Creature

I can be black,
I can be everywhere,
I scare people,
What am I?

Answer: A spider.

Harvie-James Upton (7)
St Nicholas CE (VC) Infant School, Strood

The Slow Thing

I live in a black tree,
I am slow and wee on myself,
I begin with an 's',
I climb sometimes, but lazily,
I have black and white fur,
I have sharp nails,
I live in hot places and forests,
I don't like going near people because they make fun of me,
I have four legs,
I do not have a tail,
I don't have four eyes,
What am I?

Answer: A sloth.

James John Ruffle (6)
St Peter & St Paul Catholic Primary Academy, St Paul's Cray

The Fastest African Animal

I am very fast, as fast as a train,
I have black spots all over,
I have four short legs,
I have a short tail,
I can catch my own prey, like meat,
I have short, yellow fur,
I have long whiskers,
I'm a meat eater,
I'm a predator,
I'm faster than the wind,
I belong to the cat family,
What am I?

Answer: A cheetah.

Caleb Olivier (6)
St Peter & St Paul Catholic Primary Academy, St Paul's Cray

The Fast Runner

I have black dots all over,
I am really fast at running,
I eat other animals for my meal,
I belong to the cat family,
I have a short, yellow tail,
I have yellow fur,
What am I?

Answer: A cheetah.

Isobelle Hobson McDonagh (6)
St Peter & St Paul Catholic Primary Academy, St Paul's Cray

The Family Of Pom Poms

I'm sometimes colourful and round,
You can put me in a can,
I'm fluffy and I am cuddly,
And you can squeeze me,
Sometimes I am little,
And I'm very soft,
What am I?

Answer: A pom pom.

Jasmine Ellen Powell (6)
St Peter & St Paul Catholic Primary Academy, St Paul's Cray

The Scary Creature

I am black,
I am an eight-legged insect,
I don't eat what you eat,
I walk on something you can't see,
I eat bugs,
I have a pointy thing on my mouth,
What am I?

Answer: A spider.

Mark Muthike Karimi (6)
St Peter & St Paul Catholic Primary Academy, St Paul's Cray

The Furriest Animal

I have long, long fur,
I have a black nose,
I live in a den outside in the forest,
I love eating meat,
I love the meat from a rabbit,
I have a wet nose,
What am I?

Answer: A wild dog.

Oliviia Barbashova (6)
St Peter & St Paul Catholic Primary Academy, St Paul's Cray

The Spotty Animals

I have a long neck,
I can reach leaves,
I have spots on my fur,
I have hooves like horses have hooves,
I have two small ears, but I can still hear,
What am I?

Answer: A giraffe.

Shi Yu Lin (6)
St Peter & St Paul Catholic Primary Academy, St Paul's Cray

The Fast Runner

I have whiskers,
I have four black legs,
I like lots of milk,
I have a black and brown tail,
I have black and brown eyes,
I have a furry body,
What am I?

Answer: A cat.

Camilla Ivy Maria Nangonzi Ssemanda (6)
St Peter & St Paul Catholic Primary Academy, St Paul's Cray

A Juicy Treasure

I have green seeds outside,
My seeds are small,
I have red all over me,
I have leaves at the top of me,
I have a yummy taste,
What am I?

Answer: A strawberry.

Grace Knorton (6)
St Peter & St Paul Catholic Primary Academy, St Paul's Cray

The Fast Wings

I have a pink body,
I have rainbow wings and two eyes,
I'm pink and purple,
My wings are colourful,
I fly over the pond,
What am I?

Answer: A butterfly.

Lize-Mari Nel (6)
St Peter & St Paul Catholic Primary Academy, St Paul's Cray

The Slowest Animal

I have four long legs,
I have long whiskers,
I have a long tail,
I have big eyes,
I have orange fur,
I have two small ears,
What am I?

Answer: A fox.

Michelle Stamerra (5)
St Peter & St Paul Catholic Primary Academy, St Paul's Cray

The Soft Animal

I have a short and black tail,
I love eating a mouse,
I love playing outside,
I love drinking cold milk,
I run around the house,
What am I?

Answer: A cat.

Alfie Kerry (6)
St Peter & St Paul Catholic Primary Academy, St Paul's Cray

The Plant Eater

I'm black and I'm white,
I've got striped fur,
I eat plants and fruit,
I live in a forest,
I sleep on the floor,
What am I?

Answer: A zebra.

Finley Hopkins (6)
St Peter & St Paul Catholic Primary Academy, St Paul's Cray

The Milk Drinker

I have milk and it's white,
I have whiskers,
I have four legs,
I eat food,
I catch a mouse,
I have sharp claws,
What am I?

Answer: A cat.

Kiara Chin (6)
St Peter & St Paul Catholic Primary Academy, St Paul's Cray

The Fiery Monster

I have sharp teeth,
I have tongues of fire,
I am spotty,
I am red,
I am orange,
I have wings,
What am I?

Answer: A dragon.

Henry Taylor (5)
St Peter & St Paul Catholic Primary Academy, St Paul's Cray

Ice Power!

I slide on the ice,
I don't taste nice,
I have eggs,
I have legs,
I'm not as shiny as a mirror,
My predator is a bear,
I eat fish,
In a dish,
I dive in the sea,
And say, "Charp!"
What am I?

Answer: A penguin.

Emilia Sophia Mirsadeghi (7)
Valley Invicta Primary School At Kings Hill, Kings Hill

I'm Interesting

I'm interesting and can be bought in a nice, quiet place,
I'm creative and interesting,
I'm important and can be found in a school,
I'm important and special and can be found in a library,
What am I?

Answer: A book.

Martin Neves Hajdinjak (7)
Valley Invicta Primary School At Kings Hill, Kings Hill

Ice Like Snow

I live in a cold place,
I don't need a blanket,
I live in a cove,
I have snow and ice,
It is really dark,
My home is really cold,
It snows every day,
What am I?

Answer: A penguin.

Cody Embery-Reid (7)
Valley Invicta Primary School At Kings Hill, Kings Hill

Honey

I live in the forest,
I love honey,
I am furry, but I'm not a kitten,
I live in a cave,
I hunt my prey,
I am not good at climbing,
What am I?

Answer: A bear.

Rufaro Chihlayo
Valley Invicta Primary School At Kings Hill, Kings Hill

Autumn

I am always different,
There are a lot of me,
I'm not in the sea,
I'll keep you alive,
Every year, I get a line on my spine,
What am I?

Answer: A tree.

Luca Jack Hewlett (7)
Valley Invicta Primary School At Kings Hill, Kings Hill

Colourful

I'm really colourful, as bright as the sun,
Give me to your mum,
Watch me grow,
In the wind I flow,
I smell really nice,
What am I?

Answer: A flower.

Jasmine Lara
Valley Invicta Primary School At Kings Hill, Kings Hill

Names

I have lots of letters on me,
I have someone's name on me,
I am tiny,
I can be sewn on to things,
What am I?

Answer: A label.

Thomas Miller
Valley Invicta Primary School At Kings Hill, Kings Hill

Rushing

I can kill people,
I am mainly blue, but I can be brown,
I am cold and hot,
Animals live in me,
What am I?

Answer: A river.

Alex Zilliox
Valley Invicta Primary School At Kings Hill, Kings Hill

Eight-Legged

I have not got five feet
I have more
My name is Blue
I eat little fish
What am I?

Answer: An octopus.

Zachary Harding
Valley Invicta Primary School At Kings Hill, Kings Hill

What Am I?

I leave a wet, green, gooey trail when I slide,
I look like jelly, but you would not want to gobble me up,
I'm soft and squishy,
I'm also the opposite of shiny white pearls,
I eat juicy, lovely leaves and I hide in them,
You hate me because I am always near you, destroying your garden,
What am I?

Answer: A slug.

Sydnee Mitchell (7)
Westgate Primary School, Dartford

What Am I?

I've got two long, green antennae,
I munch on yummy, delicious plants under green, smooth grass,
I bounce as high as two centimetres,
I normally sneak under smooth grass,
I make loud nosies by rubbing my back,
You will spot my shiny, bold eyes,
What am I?

Answer: A grasshopper.

Yasmine Rouabhi (7)
Westgate Primary School, Dartford

Frosty Flake

I'm as cold as anything can be,
I'm very creamy and very tasty,
People usually have me on boiling days,
I am not lucky, I melt on hot days,
If I'm not in a pot or in a cone, I'll die,
I am given to hungry people with yummy toppings,
What am I?

Answer: An ice cream.

Solah Hayat (7)
Westgate Primary School, Dartford

What Am I?

My favourite colour is red,
I love to eat sweet nectar and yummy pollen,
I can hunt up to fifty tasty aphids a day,
Inside a leaf, I'm a circle,
I'm black and you can find me inside a dark, juicy leaf,
I may have twenty spots on my red back,
What am I?

Answer: A ladybird.

Dumebi Lauren Molokwu (7)
Westgate Primary School, Dartford

Fantastic Animal

I have long legs and a long neck,
I come in different colours;
Blue, green, yellow, and sometimes red,
Just like prizes, I come in all shapes and sizes,
I have two eyes in front and 100 behind me,
I have lots of feathers, as big as they can be,
What am I?

Answer: A peacock.

Ire Sulaimon (7)
Westgate Primary School, Dartford

What Am I?

I'm furry and scary,
I come out at night, every night,
I have a fluffy, orange tail,
I have pointy, sharp, creepy teeth,
I creep on the pretty quiet streets at night,
I look for delicious food,
I have four legs and a good sense of smell,
What am I?

Answer: A fox.

Ashwina Shagindra (7)
Westgate Primary School, Dartford

What Am I?

I am very spotty,
I have very big white eyes,
My body is not white, except for my eyes,
I have wings that are as precious as red rubies,
I munch on lots of aphids, flowers and leaves,
I move gently,
What am I?

Answer: A ladybird.

Rammiya Sathiyavarathan (7)
Westgate Primary School, Dartford

The Graceful Glider

I can fly as peacefully as a dove,
But I wish I could touch the stars above,
I also wish I could fly to space,
As I can fly with so much grace,
I love to make big, puffy nests,
I also love to lay eggs,
What am I?

Answer: A bird.

Nazeeha Noor Mohamed (7)
Westgate Primary School, Dartford

Cheeky All Day

I like chasing cats, that's no treat,
I eat cheese, which I love to eat,
And I steal food that is for your pet,
I am fast in a race,
I like juggling,
I like to thump and jump,
What am I?

Answer: A mouse.

Callum Hardy (7)
Westgate Primary School, Dartford

What Am I?

I have hands,
I have a face,
But I cannot smile,
I have numbers,
But you will not see thirteen,
I am a circle,
I run, but cannot walk,
People check on me often,
What am I?

Answer: A clock.

Macey Poppy Manning (7)
Westgate Primary School, Dartford

Sweet Surprise

I'm sweet and colourful and taste beautiful,
I live in a fridge and you can put me in a cone or on a stick,
I can be small or I can be big,
People can lick me,
What am I?

Answer: An ice cream.

Lola Cousins (6)
Westgate Primary School, Dartford

The Invisible Animal

It howls in the air,
It flies anywhere,
It's very similar to air,
It makes kites fly around,
They go whirling, swirling round,
What is it?

Answer: *The wind.*

Prionti Kazi Munia (6)
Westgate Primary School, Dartford

Speedy Spots

I can catch and eat you.
I eat antelopes.
I run very fast.
I have black spots.
I live in Africa.
I am the fastest land animal.
What am I?

Answer: A cheetah.

Hester Liddicoat (6)
Westmeads Community Infant School, Whitstable

Harley

I am your best friend,
My hair will make you itch,
I will give you my paw and wag my tail,
My wet tongue will give you kisses,
I have four legs to chase you with,
I like to lie on the sofa,
What am I?

Answer: A dog.

Ruby-Rae (6)
White Cliffs Primary College For The Arts, Dover

Busy Buzz

I have stripes which are black and yellow,
I buzz around the flowers, looking for nectar for me to collect,
Sometimes I sting if I am afraid,
I love to come out when the sun is shining,
What am I?

Answer: A bee.

Kelsi H (6)
White Cliffs Primary College For The Arts, Dover

Time For Warm

Sun's up nice and early,
Trees and flowers start to grow,
People start to plan holidays,
We enjoy time at the seaside,
We all enjoy ice cream,
What is it?

Answer: Summer.

Zane Rackstraw (6)
White Cliffs Primary College For The Arts, Dover

Hot And Sunny

I am so hot,
You can go to the beach and have fun in the water,
Play in the sand and have ice cream,
Do you know people can sweat?
What am I?

Answer: Summer.

Alexander Maneshi (6)
White Cliffs Primary College For The Arts, Dover

Fruity

I start as a flower,
I grow on a tree,
You can find me in a shop,
My colour is red or green,
I'm also very healthy,
What am I?

Answer: An apple.

Grace Leigh Broster (6)
White Cliffs Primary College For The Arts, Dover

Love

Everybody has one,
Some are small,
Some are big,
But we love them all,
We have so much fun,
What are we?

Answer: A family.

Eleanor-Rose Mctaggart (5)
White Cliffs Primary College For The Arts, Dover

YoungWriters
Est.1991

YOUNG WRITERS INFORMATION

We hope you have enjoyed reading this book – and that you will continue to in the coming years.

If you're a young writer who enjoys reading and creative writing, or the parent of an enthusiastic poet or story writer, do visit our website www.youngwriters.co.uk. Here you will find free competitions, workshops and games, as well as recommended reads, a poetry glossary and our blog.

If you would like to order further copies of this book, or any of our other titles, then please give us a call or visit www.youngwriters.co.uk.

Young Writers
Remus House
Coltsfoot Drive
Peterborough
PE2 9BF
(01733) 890066
info@youngwriters.co.uk